THIS IS
BABY

To my babies: Winnie, Franny, and Nancy.
And to my mom—I finally get it. And I'm enjoying every second.

A FEIWEL AND FRIENDS BOOK
An imprint of Macmillan Publishing Group, LLC
120 Broadway, New York, NY 10271

Our books may be purchased in bulk for promotional, educational, or business use.
Please contact your local bookseller or the Macmillan Corporate and Premium Sales Department at
(800) 221-7945 ext. 5442 or by email at MacmillanSpecialMarkets@macmillan.com.

Library of Congress Cataloging-in-Publication Data is available.

ISBN 978-1-250-24560-1

Book design by Rich Deas and Miguel Ordóñez

Feiwel and Friends logo designed by Filomena Tuosto

First edition, 2019

1 3 5 7 9 10 8 6 4 2

mackids.com

THIS IS
BABY

JIMMY FALLON

ILLUSTRATED BY
MIGUEL ORDÓÑEZ

FEIWEL AND FRIENDS
NEW YORK

This is BABY.

Let's laugh and play and sing!

What are the parts of BABY?

Well, I'll tell you EVERYTHING!

These are BABY's **EYES.**

This is BABY's **NOSE.**

These are BABY's **FINGERS.**

These are BABY's TOES.

This is your **HEAD.**

This is your **HAIR.**

This is a hat

that you put on there!

These are BABY's EARS.

These are BABY's **LIPS.**

These are BABY's **KNEES.**

These are BABY's **HIPS.**

This is BABY's **TUMMY.**

And if tickling is a problem . . .

Just turn BABY over, and this is BABY's

These are BABY's **ELBOWS.**

These are BABY's shrugging. **SHOULDERS**

These are BABY's **ARMS**

that are made for super-hugging!

There are so many parts of BABY.

HAIR

KNEE

HIP

SHOULDER

EYES

HEAD

ELBOW

EAR

These are just the things we see.

But the biggest part of BABY

is the **LOVE** you get from **ME.**

QUACK!